Secret
in the
Attic

Peril at the Pyramids

by **L. A. Peacock**
illustrated by **Nathan Hale**

Scholastic Inc.
New York   Toronto   London   Auckland
Sydney   Mexico City   New Delhi   Hong Kong

To Owen and Hayden Teasdale,
my reading buddies, with love
— L.A.F.

ISBN 978-0-545-24766-5

Text copyright © 2011 by L. A. Peacock
Illustrations copyright © 2011 by Scholastic Inc.

12 11 10 9 8 7 6 5 4 3 2 1   11 12 13 14 15 16/0

Printed in the U.S.A.   40

First Scholastic printing, January 2011

Chapter 1

The Dark Attic

"It's raining," Jess said.

Heavy rain was pounding on the windows. It was early morning, but the sky was dark.

Slowly, Josh opened his eyes.

Jess stood next to his bed. She was wearing a shiny red raincoat.

"Get up, sleepyhead," she ordered. "Time for school." Jess liked to boss around her ten-year-old twin brother.

"Oh, man," said Josh, rubbing his eyes.

Jess pulled away the covers. She handed Josh his rain slicker. A flashlight was in her other hand.

"Come on," said Jess. "The rubber boots are in the attic. They belonged to Dad and Uncle Harry."

She ran out of the room to the end of the hall. A rope was hanging from the ceiling. Jess grabbed the rope and pulled. The wooden ladder to the attic dropped down.

Josh jumped out of bed. He pulled on jeans and a T-shirt. Sneakers next.

"Hey, wait for me!" Josh rushed down the hall.

Jess stood on the top step of the ladder. Her brother was behind her.

"Push hard," said Josh. Sometimes the old door in the ceiling got stuck.

Jess shoved, and the door opened. She peeked in. The attic was dark. She remembered the last time the twins had been in the attic. Strange things happened in this old house.

Jess stepped back. "You go in first."

"Afraid of ghosts?" Josh laughed. His sister read a lot of scary mysteries.

Josh took the flashlight from Jess and turned it on. He saw the rain boots in the corner, next to an old trunk.

There it was—Uncle Harry's old trunk. It was covered with stickers from all over the world. Their uncle had disappeared four years earlier on one of his trips.

"Hey," said Jess. "That old trunk is back in the corner!" The same trunk they had pulled over to the window a few weeks before!

"Uncle Harry was here!" Josh cried out, stepping into the attic. A big smile spread across his face. He was thinking about their last adventure.

Their uncle was an explorer and time traveler. He left a time-compass in the old trunk when he needed their help. The mysterious device had taken the twins back in time to ancient Crete.

"Remember the labyrinth?" said Josh.

Jess nodded. How could she forget? Uncle Harry had been trapped in the giant maze. The twins had saved him from the deadly Minotaur.

They leaned over the old trunk. Jess held the flashlight while Josh raised the lid.

"There's Uncle Harry's journal!" The light was on a brown leather book.

Josh pulled out the journal. The pages were filled with maps, drawings, and notes in his uncle's handwriting.

He turned to the last entry. "Look at this map."

A long wavy line showed the Nile River. Drawings of the Great Pyramid and the Great Sphinx were marked on the west bank of the river. The Valley of the Kings was to the south.

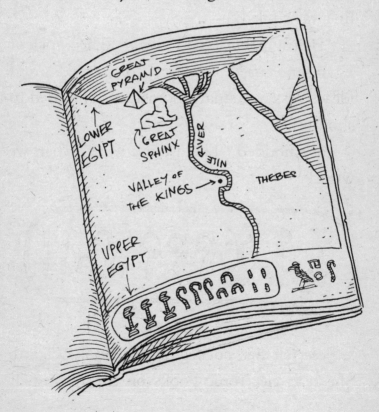

"Ancient Egypt," said Jess. "Egyptian kings called pharaohs built the pyramids." Their class had studied pyramids and mummies the year before.

"There's more." Josh pointed to some strange marks at the bottom of the page. One line was circled.

"Hieroglyphs," said Jess. "The ancient Egyptians used pictures for sounds and ideas." Jess was smart. Sometimes she tried to show off.

Josh nodded. "Like we use words when we write."

Jess felt her pocket for the Book Wizard. She read electronic books on the Wizard. It helped her look up all kinds of facts, too.

She clicked on the Wizard's encyclopedia. Then Jess typed in H-I-E-R-O-G-L-Y-P-H-S and selected "ancient Egypt." A dictionary of hieroglyphs appeared on the screen.

NUMBER	HIEROGLYPH	PICTURE
1		STROKE
10		CATTLE YOKE
100		ROPE
1000		LOTUS PLANT

"Those hieroglyphs are numbers," said Jess. "The Egyptians counted like we do, on base ten. You know, like one, ten, one hundred."

Josh studied the hieroglyph that was circled. Was it a clue to set the time-compass?

"There are three lotus plants," said Josh.

"That must mean three thousand," said Jess, glancing at the Wizard screen. Josh wrote the number 3,000 in the journal.

"And three rope pictures, three cattle-yoke pictures, and four strokes. That's three hundred thirty-four," Jess said, counting.

Josh added the numbers 300, 30, and 4 to 3,000. The sum was 3,334. He marked the total in the journal.

"What else is in the trunk?" asked Jess.

Josh leaned in and grabbed something from the corner.

"Uncle Harry's leather bag!" said Jess. She took it from Josh. A heavy metal thing was inside. *The time-compass.*

They stared at the strange device. It had hands like a clock. A third hand showed direction: N, S, E, or W.

"Something is different," said Jess. She pointed to the number marks on the time-compass. They looked like hieroglyphs.

"Cool!" said Josh. "Ancient Egypt!" Uncle Harry had left them the time-compass. And they had the time: 3,334 years earlier. They were going on a new adventure.

"No way!" said Jess, shaking her head. Ancient Egypt was a dangerous place.

Jess started to walk away.

"Wait!" Josh grabbed her arm. "Maybe there's more."

He picked up the leather bag and turned it upside down. A package dropped out. Something was wrapped in stiff brown paper. Two small objects fell to the floor.

"Look at these statues!" said Jess. She held the small golden figures in the light. One looked like a snake. The other was a bird. Jess turned to show Josh.

But her brother was busy. He was moving the hands of the time-compass.

"Hey, what are you doing?" she asked.

"Setting the time-compass." Josh was

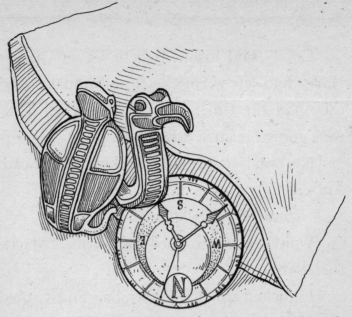

matching the hieroglyph in the journal with the marks on the time-compass.

"Are you nuts?" said Jess.

Josh looked up. "Uncle Harry must be in trouble."

Jess was quiet. Josh was right. Their uncle needed their help.

The time-compass was set to 3,334, back in time more than three thousand years!

"Wait!" shouted Jess. She picked up the Wizard and the brown paper. Quickly, she threw them into the leather bag with the two gold statues.

"Are you sure you want to go with me?" asked Josh. Sometimes Jess got scared.

Jess nodded. Josh couldn't go alone. They were a team.

"Let's go!" she said.

Josh grabbed the journal.

The time-compass was making clicking sounds. They were getting louder and louder.

The floor of the attic was shaking.

Jess held tightly to Josh.

A bright light flashed.

The time-compass was sending them to ancient Egypt!

Chapter 2

The Three Pyramids

Josh opened his eyes and looked around.

"Amazing!" he said. Three giant pyramids stood in the distance.

"Wow!" Jess shaded her eyes. They were in the middle of the desert.

The sun felt hot. Josh touched the top of his head.

"Hey, what happened to my hair?" said Josh. His hair was missing on one side. On the other side, a pigtail was hanging over his ear.

Jess stared at her brother. Josh was wearing a white linen kilt and sandals. A colorful necklace of glass beads covered his bare shoulders.

His jeans, T-shirt, and sneakers were gone.

"You're bald," said Jess. She giggled. "And you have black paint around your eyes."

"You have black makeup on your eyes, too," said Josh. He looked down at his bare legs. "We look like ancient Egyptian kids."

Jess wore a pleated white dress and sandals. Her long hair was combed into tiny braids with beads on the ends. Magically, their clothes had changed.

The time-compass had taken Jess and Josh to ancient Egypt, but where exactly?

Jess reached into Uncle Harry's leather bag. She pulled out the Book Wizard and turned it on. She entered some keywords.

"That's the Great Sphinx, next to the pyramids," said Jess. She pointed to a large stone statue in the distance. It had the body of a lion and the head of a man.

Josh opened Uncle Harry's journal.

"Type in the word 'pyramids' and this place," said Josh. He spelled "Giza." His finger was on the map.

Jess read:

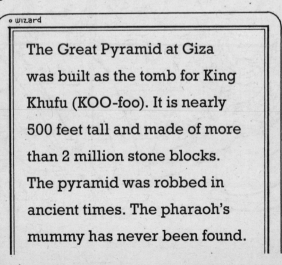

o Wizard

The Great Pyramid at Giza
was built as the tomb for King
Khufu (KOO-foo). It is nearly
500 feet tall and made of more
than 2 million stone blocks.
The pyramid was robbed in
ancient times. The pharaoh's
mummy has never been found.

"Cool," said Josh. "Maybe Uncle Harry is looking for the stolen mummy."

Jess made a face. "Yuck!" She didn't want to look for a dead body.

"Or he's looking for treasure," said Josh. "The ancient Egyptians buried gold and jewelry with their mummies."

"Maybe," said Jess.

Uncle Harry had found a sacred tablet in Crete. It had been stolen from an ancient Greek temple. The twins had helped Uncle Harry return the lost tablet to its true owner.

Jess remembered the package in the leather bag. She pulled out the golden statues of the snake and the bird. The brown paper fell to the ground.

She held up the strange objects.

"Where did Uncle Harry find these little statues?" Jess asked.

Josh picked up the brown paper and turned it over. Hieroglyphs were painted on one side of the paper.

"Four new picture clues," said Josh.

Jess glanced at the hieroglyphs. "Maybe Uncle Harry sent us a message." She turned on the Wizard and called up the dictionary of hieroglyphs.

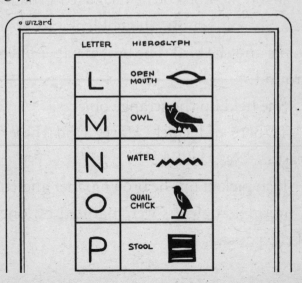

LETTER	HIEROGLYPH	
L	OPEN MOUTH	
M	OWL	
N	WATER	
O	QUAIL CHICK	
P	STOOL	

Josh pointed at the picture writing. Shelter. Vulture. Open mouth. Stool.

He studied the dictionary. Each picture represented a sound. He wrote the letters in the journal.

"Okay," said Jess. "So what do they mean?"

"It's a message from Uncle Harry, all right," said Josh. "The shelter symbol stands for 'h,' the vulture for 'e' . . ."

"And the open mouth for 'l,'" said Jess.

Josh looked up. "And the stool for . . . 'p.'"

"HELP!" said the twins together.

Chapter 3

The Lost Dog

Josh looked around. The three pyramids seemed far away. There were no roads, just hills of sand. Up ahead were some palm trees and a patch of tall grass.

"Where to now?" asked Jess. The desert was hot, and she was thirsty.

Josh wasn't sure. They needed a plan.

"Let's go there," said Josh, pointing to the trees. "The river must be nearby."

Jess groaned. She looked down at her sandals. The sand was hot.

"Come on," said Josh, grabbing her hand.

* * *

An hour later, the twins sat down in the shade of a big palm tree. A leather cup was hanging next to a well. They drank the cool water. The sound of the waves splashing on the riverbank made them sleepy.

A loud bark woke them.

A big black dog was standing in front of Jess. The dog's coat was shiny. Around his neck was a gold collar with sparkling jewels.

The dog barked again. Then he leaned over to Jess and nuzzled against her leg.

"What's your name, pretty boy?" asked Jess. She scratched the silky fur behind the dog's ears.

Josh leaned over. He looked at the dog's fancy gold collar.

"I wonder who he belongs to." Maybe the owner was looking for his dog right now.

"He's beautiful," said Jess.

Suddenly, the dog started to walk away. Then he looked back at the twins.

"I think he wants us to follow him," said Josh. The dog ran down a path between the trees, toward the river. Josh was right behind him.

"Hey, wait for me," shouted Jess. She grabbed Uncle Harry's leather bag and took off after Josh.

The grass along the river was tall and thick. Jess looked around. Maybe there were crocodiles or other dangerous animals.

A loud shriek broke the silence. Some strange birds were flying over the river.

Several loud roars followed. There were more wild animals out there.

"Josh!" called Jess. "Where are we going?" She was scared. This was not a safe place.

The dog stopped at a sandy spot on the riverbank. Small boats were tied to a wooden dock. The boats were flat. They were made of reeds held together with ropes.

Jess and Josh heard voices. They hid behind the tall grass and listened. They could understand the strange language. It was magic, like the time-travel device.

"I think they're hunters," said Josh. He stood up to get a better look. They were mostly young boys. Some had spears. Others were carrying bows and arrows.

"They're talking about . . . 'the big one,'" said Jess. *Must be some kind of animal.*

"Wait here," said Josh. He moved closer to the hunters. He could hear clearly now.

"Hippopotamus . . ." They were hippo hunters!

Josh turned and looked back at Jess. His face froze.

Behind her was the strange dog.

By the dog's side was a tall Egyptian boy staring at them. A boy holding a spear.

Chapter 4

The Hippo Hunt

Jess looked up at Josh. "What's wrong?"

Josh stared at the boy behind Jess. He wore a white linen kilt and black eye paint. A gold band held his pigtail to one side.

"Hello," said Josh. "We . . . er . . . found your dog." He could speak the strange language. More magic from the time-compass.

The dog leaned over Jess's shoulder. He licked her face.

Jess laughed. She hugged the big dog. Then she looked behind her.

"What's his name?" she asked the boy. She could speak the strange language, too.

The Egyptian boy put down his spear. "His name is Nubis. He likes you."

Jess held out her hand. "I'm Jess," she said. "That's my brother, Josh."

"I'm Amun," he answered. "Welcome. Are you here to join the hunt?" He gave his spear to Josh.

"Er . . . ," said Josh as he took the spear. "We got here this morning." He didn't know what to say.

The spear felt light. Josh held it over his shoulder, like a football. Josh was good at sports. He pumped the spear like he was throwing a forward pass.

Amun talked about yesterday's hunt. A bull hippo had escaped. Several hunters were hurt. They needed Josh's help.

Yikes! Josh thought. This was no football game. Josh looked at Jess.

Jess stepped back and turned on the Wizard. She hid behind the tall grass and searched for "hippo hunting" on the Wizard's encyclopedia.

There were loud noises coming from the river. Some boys were waving to Amun.

"Bring the boats," shouted Amun, running toward the dock.

The hunt was about to begin.

Josh rushed to Jess. They hunched over the Wizard's screen.

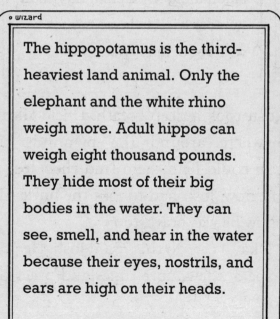

The hippopotamus is the third-heaviest land animal. Only the elephant and the white rhino weigh more. Adult hippos can weigh eight thousand pounds. They hide most of their big bodies in the water. They can see, smell, and hear in the water because their eyes, nostrils, and ears are high on their heads.

"They're *really* big," said Josh.

Jess clicked to the next screen.

o Wizard

Hippos are dangerous. They
can easily flip over small boats.
Hunters keep the wind behind
them, because hippos hide
under the water when they
smell danger. Ancient Egyptian
hunters tried to lasso hippos
with rope, then spear them.

Josh took a deep breath. Uncle Harry was somewhere around the pyramids. Maybe Amun could help them find their lost uncle. Right now, Josh had to join the hunt. He had to show he was brave, too.

"Okay, I can do this," said Josh. He pumped the spear a few more times and practiced his throw.

Jess shook her head. "Bad idea," she said as they headed toward the river. This was not a good plan.

The hunters pushed reed boats into the water and jumped on. Amun was standing in a small boat. A heavy rope was coiled at his feet.

Josh untied a reed boat and stepped in. It rocked back and forth with the waves.

"Lean on your spear! Balance the boat!" called Jess. She gave the boat a big push. Then she sat on the riverbank next to Nubis.

The small boat moved quickly in the Nile current. Josh floated his boat alongside Amun's.

A pod of hippos was just ahead. Only the tops of their heads, with their wide nostrils and bulging eyes, were above the water. The hunters were trying to move the big bull hippo away from the others.

The bull hippo was angry. He opened his giant mouth, showing his sharp teeth. He let out a big roar. The hunters moved closer with their bows and spears. The attack was on.

"Follow me!" Amun yelled to Josh. The bull hippo was swimming their way.

Amun moved his boat to the left of the charging hippo. Josh was right behind him.

In his left hand, Amun held the rope. With his right hand, he made a loop. Amun spun the lasso above his head. Then he tossed the rope around the hippo's neck.

Caught in the rope, the hippo roared louder. He swung his huge head back and forth, trying to throw off the lasso.

The other hunters were closing in on both sides.

Amun twisted the rope around his wrists. Then he pulled with all his strength.

Suddenly, the hippo took in air and closed his mouth. He dived deep into the water, taking the rope with him. The rope jerked in

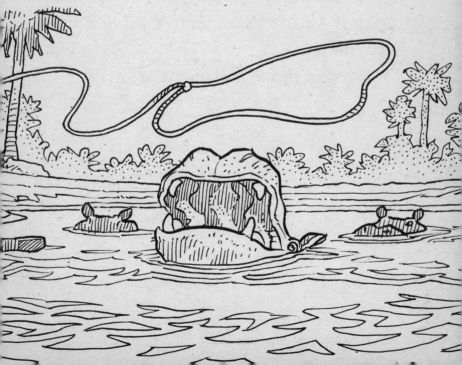

Amun's hands. Amun fell out of his boat into the murky water of the Nile.

"Amun!" shouted Josh. "Let go of the rope!" He watched Amun being dragged under the water.

Josh looked around. The other hunters were far away. He threw down his spear, took a deep breath, and dived into the water.

The bull hippo was at the bottom of the river. Amun was trying to untie the rope from his wrist. He was running out of air. Josh grabbed Amun's hands and pulled him free from the rope.

Together, they kicked up to the surface.

Chapter 5

Grave Robbers

Josh and Amun floated toward the riverbank. Nubis jumped into the water and splashed toward the boys.

Amun hung on to Nubis's collar until they reached the shore. Jess pulled Amun onto the riverbank. There was a spear a few feet away. She picked it up and ran to the water's edge.

"Josh! Josh!" cried Jess. "Grab this spear." She held on to one end and pulled Josh out of the water. He rolled over on the wet grass next to Amun.

"Wow!" said Josh. He pointed to the river. The hunters were pulling the huge body of the hippo out of the water. Amun's rope was around the big head. Arrows and spears were stuck deep in the hippo's thick skin.

Amun shook his head and laughed. "We got the big one after all!"

He turned to Josh and Jess. "Thank you, my friends."

Amun took something sparkling from his neck and handed it to Jess.

"It's beautiful," she said. Jess held the blue glass in the light. It was flat and oval shaped. Hieroglyphs were carved on one side.

"Look," Jess said. She turned to show Josh. But her brother was ahead, walking through the tall grass. Jess tied the blue glass around her neck.

"Come," said Amun. "We need dry clothes and food to eat."

It was almost dark when they reached the hunters' camp. Servants were busy making dinner. Women washed dates and figs in clay bowls. Some men cleaned fish and cooked them on hot flat stones.

Large white tents stood among the palm trees. Guards were standing next to horses and chariots. The biggest guard stared at Josh and Jess. A mean look was on his face. He was the captain.

The huge guard grabbed his spear and ran toward them.

"Stop!" he shouted. The other guards made a circle around Josh and Jess.

"What do *you* want?" asked Jess boldly. She looked into the captain's eyes.

"Now we're in trouble," said Josh. He turned around.

Amun was right behind them.

The young Egyptian raised his arm.

"Put down your weapons!" he ordered. "These are my friends."

The guards lowered their spears. They bowed their heads to Amun. The captain gave Jess a long, hard look.

"He looks mean," whispered Jess. "And he doesn't like strangers."

Josh looked around. Bows and arrows. Spears. Chariots. Horses. This was more than a hunters' camp. These boys were training to be soldiers.

Two servants rushed over and stood in front of them. They held bowls of water and soft towels.

"Wash," said Amun, handing towels to Jess and Josh. He gave more orders. The servants ran to get clean clothes.

Josh and Jess walked with Amun toward the largest tent. The desert was all around them.

The three pyramids were in the distance.

Jess looked around. Maybe Uncle Harry was trapped in one of the pyramids.

Suddenly, loud noises and shouts came from behind them. Josh turned. The guards were dragging some men. The men were tied together with a long rope.

The captain rushed over and grabbed the rope.

"Move!" he ordered, giving the last man a push with his spear.

Jess was puzzled. She turned to Amun. "Who are those men?"

"Grave robbers," said Amun. "The pyramids were built a thousand years ago. And still evil men try to steal the treasures."

Jess reached into the leather bag. She felt the two golden statues. *Did these sacred objects come from a pharaoh's grave? Did Uncle Harry take them?*

The prisoners walked past, one by one.

"Look for Uncle Harry," Josh whispered.

Jess stared at the faces. Her heart was beating wildly.

"Whew!" she sighed as the last tomb robber marched by.

Uncle Harry wasn't there.

Chapter 6

At Camp

The twins sat down to dinner on reed mats with Amun and the hunters. Figs and dates were served first. Then they shared dishes of cooked meat and fish. Sweet wine and honey cakes were served throughout the meal.

Suddenly, Josh noticed the mean captain staring at them.

"Be careful of *him*," Josh said quietly to Jess.

"He doesn't like us," Jess whispered. She gazed into the man's beady eyes. A twisted grin fell across his face.

"Yeah," said Josh. "He's a bully." Amun was

telling stories about the hippo hunt. A linen headcloth covered his hair. A gold headband with the figure of a snake held it in place.

Jess stared at Amun's gold band. The snake looked like the sacred figure from the attic trunk. It was in their leather bag. The strange bird statue was in there, too.

Amun reached up and touched the gold snake. "This uraeus gives me power," he said. "The cobra goddess protects me when I hunt. She will protect me in the afterlife, too. I am not afraid of death."

The servants cleared the last dishes. Then they brought out a fancy board game.

"Challenge!" shouted Amun. He handed a set of counters and throw sticks to one of the hunters. The captain moved in closer to watch the players.

"Oh, man," whispered Josh. "How do we play *that*?"

"Wait," said Jess. "I'll look it up."

Jess and Josh moved to the side. Jess turned on the Wizard and searched for "ancient Egyptian board game."

"It looks easy," said Jess. She was on the chess team at school.

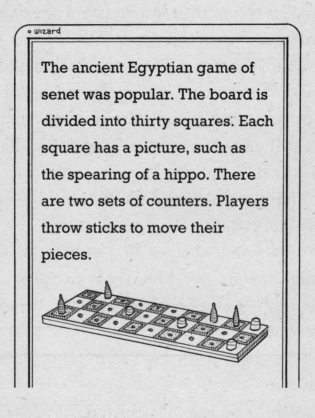

o Wizard

The ancient Egyptian game of senet was popular. The board is divided into thirty squares. Each square has a picture, such as the spearing of a hippo. There are two sets of counters. Players throw sticks to move their pieces.

"Yeah," said Josh. "Bet you can beat him." Jess was the best at board games.

They sat behind the hunters and watched

the moves. Amun won the first three games. The captain lost the last game.

"Who is next to challenge me?" asked Amun. He laughed and nodded to Jess. "My sister is a good player. Are you?"

"You're on!" cried Jess.

The captain growled. His eyes followed Jess as she sat opposite Amun. Josh set up the senet pieces.

"You move first," said Jess politely. She bowed her head to Amun.

Amun threw the sticks and moved some pieces.

Jess stared at the board. She looked for a path between Amun's pieces. Then she threw the sticks and made her move. It was a good one. She removed two of Amun's pieces from the board.

"Go, Jess!" shouted Josh. The hunters cheered for Jess, too. Only the captain looked angry.

Amun laughed. Girls were good players in his family, too.

They played senet until midnight. Jess won most of her games.

It was late when Amun left Jess and Josh at a small tent.

Tomorrow was a big day. Ostrich hunting. With horses and chariots.

"Yikes," said Jess, climbing onto her sleeping mat. "Did you hear that? Ostrich hunting!"

Josh shook his head. No more hunting for him. "We leave tomorrow morning."

"Right," said Jess. That captain was giving her the creeps. And it was time to find their uncle.

The fire outside the tent kept away the cool desert air. They fell asleep as soon as their heads touched the mats.

Just before dawn, Josh woke up to a strange sound. Someone with a knife was outside — cutting an opening in their tent!

Chapter 7

Escape to the River

Josh reached over and shook Jess.

"What . . . ?" Jess said.

"Shhh!" Josh pointed to a shadow on the side of the tent. It was of a man holding a knife!

"The captain?" whispered Jess. She was frightened.

Josh grabbed a spear. He pushed Jess behind him.

The knife ripped through the thick cloth. A man stepped through the opening. He wore the tunic and leather vest of an Egyptian soldier.

Jess held her breath.

When Josh saw the man's face, he grinned.

"Uncle Harry!" cried Jess.

She jumped up and gave her uncle a big hug.

They left the tent quietly. Nubis was outside. He rubbed against Jess, then walked back toward Amun's tent.

"That's Nubis," said Jess sadly. She would miss her friend.

Uncle Harry stared at the big black dog. *Anubis, protector god of the pharaohs!*

The camp was quiet. Everyone was asleep, including the guards. Soon it would be dawn.

Josh handed the leather bag to his uncle.

"Where are we going?" Josh asked. Except for his unusual clothes, Uncle Harry looked the same. His long hair was pulled back into a ponytail.

"Why did you leave the gold statues in the trunk?" asked Jess. "Where did they come from?"

"I'll explain later," Uncle Harry whispered. "We need to get to the river."

They crept past the big white tents and sleeping guards. Finally, the last palm tree was behind them.

For more than an hour, they traveled along the sand dunes. The first light of dawn was breaking across the desert. Ahead were a patch of high grass and the river.

They heard the shrieks of wild birds, then the sounds of the waves along the shore.

Uncle Harry and Josh rushed to the riverbank.

"Come on!" Josh waved for Jess to hurry.

The sun was up. People were starting to move along the river.

A small wooden boat was tied to the dock.

Uncle Harry untied the rope and stepped in. At the back was a rudder post with a single oar for steering. A large rectangular sail was in the middle.

Jess ran through the tall grass down to the

dock. Josh was already in the boat.

"Is this your boat?" asked Jess, grabbing her uncle's hand.

Uncle Harry shook his head and laughed. "Don't worry! I'm not a thief. I'll bring it back later."

Josh looked all around him. "Where are we going?"

"Upper Egypt," answered Uncle Harry. "Josh, grab the rudder," he ordered. "Turn the oar sideways and steer into the river. Jess, help me raise the sail."

Slowly, the boat moved upstream.

It was almost noon. The waves lapped against the sides of the boat. While Josh steered, Uncle Harry made notes in his journal.

Jess shaded her eyes. The light from the sun bounced off the blue glass necklace. She looked down at her gift from Amun. She gazed at the strange picture writing carved on one side.

The Wizard was in her pocket. Jess took it out and searched for "ancient Egyptian jewelry." She clicked through the screens. She found a glass stone with hieroglyphs.

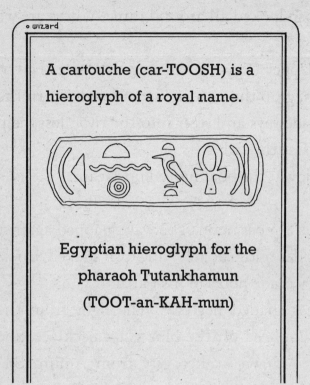

A cartouche (car-TOOSH) is a hieroglyph of a royal name.

Egyptian hieroglyph for the pharaoh Tutankhamun (TOOT-an-KAH-mun)

Jess removed the blue stone from her neck. She placed it next to the Wizard's screen. The cartouche was the same.

"Look!" Jess cried out. "This necklace belongs to King Tut." Jess knew the famous story of the boy king Tutankhamun. He had died at an early age.

Uncle Harry helped Josh tie the rudder in place. They sat next to Jess, staring at the Wizard screen.

"Amun gave me this blue stone," said Jess. She placed the necklace in Uncle Harry's hand.

"Tutankhamun. Is that Amun's real name? Is he King Tut?" asked Josh.

"But he's only a boy," said Jess, shaking her head. *Too young to be the pharaoh.*

"Tell us," said Josh, staring at his uncle. "Why are we here?"

Uncle Harry returned the necklace to Jess. The leather bag and journal were at his feet.

The journal was opened to the page with the map of Egypt. Uncle Harry traced his finger along the Nile River.

"We were at Giza," said their uncle. "That's

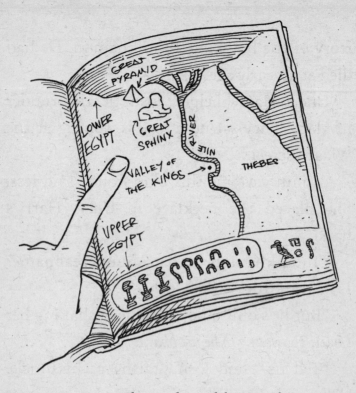

Lower Egypt. Where the Old Kingdom pyra-mids were built."

"Amun's hunting camp was there," said Josh. "Near the three pyramids."

"Right," said Uncle Harry. "It's where young pharaohs are trained to be soldiers and hunters. That's why Tutankhamun—your friend Amun — was there. That's why *I* was there."

Jess gasped. So Amun was really King Tut!

"You knew," said Josh to Uncle Harry. "About Amun?"

Harry nodded. "We're here now," he said. He moved his finger along the river toward Upper Egypt. "We want to go there, to the Valley of the Kings." He pointed to a city called Thebes.

"Hey," said Josh. "That's where they bury the pharaohs. Archaeologists found mummies in the tombs."

"Is King Tut's tomb in the Valley of the Kings?" asked Jess. She was getting a bad feeling about this.

Uncle Harry opened the leather bag. He pulled out the two gold statues. The snake and the bird figures shone in the bright sunlight.

"I found these statues in an old Greek

temple," said their uncle. "They were stolen long ago by tomb robbers and taken from Egypt."

"Who do they belong to?" asked Josh. Uncle Harry traveled in time. He returned precious objects to their true owners.

"I think I know," said Jess. "They belong to Amun. *Tutankhamun*." She remembered the gold snake on Amun's headband.

"These statues fit on Tut's mummy mask," said Uncle Harry. "We need to return them before they bury the king's mummy and seal the tomb."

Jess knew that the mask was important.

"The afterlife," said Jess. "Ancient Egyptians believe that Amun will need the mask to make the journey to the next life."

Uncle Harry nodded. "Egyptians believe that the spirit, or *ka,* of the person lives on after death. The mummy's body carries the spirit to the afterlife."

Josh shook his head. "But Amun's alive!" he said. "He's with the other hunters today. At the ostrich hunt."

"Right," said Uncle Harry. "That's because we came back too early in time. I set the time-compass to the wrong year."

He picked up the leather bag and pulled out the time-compass.

"Get ready," said their uncle. "We're going to time jump."

Jess and Josh looked at each other.

A chill ran down Jess's back.

Looking at notes in his journal, Uncle Harry moved the hands of the time-compass. Then he flipped a switch on the side.

Josh leaned in closer. He watched his uncle set the new date. Ten years ahead.

"Time jump!" cried Jess, shaking her head. They were on a boat in the middle of the Nile River. Crocodiles were crawling on the bank. Pods of hippos swam with the current.

This was not a good place to time jump.

Jess heard the familiar clicking sound of the time-compass.

"Hang on!" shouted Uncle Harry.

Josh and Jess wrapped their arms around the sail post.

The boat was rocking back and forth. The waves were getting higher and higher.

There was a sudden flash of light.

Chapter 8

Valley of the Kings

Josh opened his eyes. The riverbanks were dry. The desert reached out for miles on each side of the river.

"Wow, this part of the Nile looks different!"

"Yeah, no crocodiles or hippos," said Jess, shading her eyes from the sun. There wasn't a wild animal anywhere.

"We've come to the Valley of the Kings," called Uncle Harry from the back of the boat. The time-jump had sent them ten years forward. And to Upper Egypt.

Turning the rudder, Uncle Harry steered

toward the riverbank. The docks were crowded with people and cargo boats.

Jess reached for the Wizard. She typed in some keywords and clicked Search.

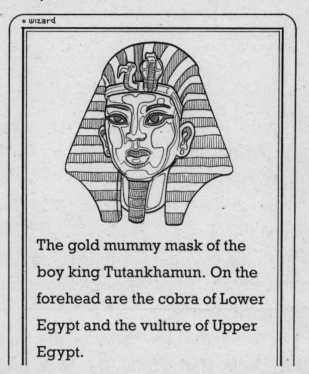

The gold mummy mask of the boy king Tutankhamun. On the forehead are the cobra of Lower Egypt and the vulture of Upper Egypt.

"What's up?" Josh sat down beside Jess. He glanced at the Wizard screen. "Is that Amun's mummy mask?"

Jess nodded. "Look at the headband." She pointed to the snake and bird figures.

"Don't you see?" cried Jess. "We have to help Uncle Harry return the statues. Amun can't pass to the afterlife until his mask is complete."

"Oh, man," said Josh. The statues in Uncle Harry's leather bag were real! They had to find Tut's tomb and return the missing statues. But how?

"Find out more about Amun." Josh wanted to know what had happened to their friend.

Jess typed in T-U-T-A-N-K-H-A-M-U-N and clicked on Search.

```
o wizard
```

King Tutankhamun was about twenty years old when he died. Scientists studied his mummy. The young king had head and leg injuries. Some believe he fell from his chariot. Maybe he died from a hunting accident.

"Oh, no," said Jess. She held the blue stone necklace tightly and thought about her friend.

"Check the Wizard for Tut's tomb and the Valley of the Kings," said Josh. The boat was headed there now.

Jess typed in some words and clicked Search.

Tutankhamun's tomb was found by the archaeologist Howard Carter in 1922. Weapons, jewelry, clothes, food, furniture, and other objects that the young pharaoh would need in the afterlife had been buried with the king's mummy. Everything was there when Carter entered the tomb.

"I guess Tut was lucky," said Jess. "The tomb robbers didn't steal his stuff."

"Yeah," said Josh. But somebody long ago had robbed the gold statues from the mask.

They had a mission now. To help Uncle Harry find Tut's mummy mask and return the gold statues. Before the tomb was sealed.

Uncle Harry guided the boat to the riverbank and tied it to the dock.

People were busy unloading boats. Large wooden sleds carried stone blocks, wood planks, tools, and other building supplies from the docks. Some workers led wagons pulled by pairs of oxen.

Uncle Harry pointed to the far side of the river. A village of mud-brick houses was in the distance.

"That's the east side of the Nile. Where the workers live," said Uncle Harry. "They build the tombs of the kings."

"Do we go to that town?" asked Jess. She wanted a hot bath and some food.

"No," said Uncle Harry. He looked at the map in his journal. "We're on the west bank. The royal tombs are located on this side of the river."

He pointed across the desert. To the Valley of the Kings.

In the distance, Jess and Josh saw tall cliff walls. Dozens of workers were cutting stone blocks out of the solid rock. Other workers were carrying supplies along the rock ledges. Tunnels were carved into the walls.

"Cool." Josh whistled. "The royal tombs!"

"Yeah," said Jess. "All we have to do is climb those cliffs."

"Let's go," said Uncle Harry. He headed off the dock. Josh was right behind him.

Jess sighed. She ran to catch up.

The road to the Valley of the Kings was crowded with wagons and sleds. It was hot. Dust was blowing everywhere.

"Uncle Harry," cried Jess. "Look at that!"

Just ahead was a special wagon decorated with gold paint and pulled by white oxen. A line of men walked behind the wagon.

They carried gold statues of gods and large metal jars. Smoke was coming from some of the jars.

"Is it a parade?" asked Josh. The smoke made the air smell sweet.

"No, those men are priests," said Uncle Harry. "It's a funeral procession. Smell the incense."

Jess pointed to the long box on the wagon.

"Is that a coffin?" she asked. On the sides, rows of hieroglyphs were painted in gold.

Uncle Harry nodded.

The procession rounded the corner and entered a large stone building.

It was the place where mummies were made.

Chapter 9

The Mummy Workshop

They stood by the door of the House of the Dead.

"Yikes!" said Jess. "Are there real mummies inside?"

"Yeah!" cried Josh. "Come on." Uncle Harry was up ahead.

"Forget it," said Jess. "It's creepy."

She didn't want to go in. But Josh pulled her along.

At the entrance, Uncle Harry turned to Jess and Josh.

"You two stay here. Keep out of trouble," he warned. "Let me find out about Tut." Maybe the king's mummy was inside.

Slowly, their uncle moved behind the funeral wagon and disappeared into the dark hallway.

"Great," said Josh. He wanted to see the mummies, not stay behind.

The twins hid behind a large clay jar. The entrance hall was empty now.

"Okay, show me what we're missing," said Josh.

Jess pulled out the Wizard. She searched for "ancient Egyptian mummies."

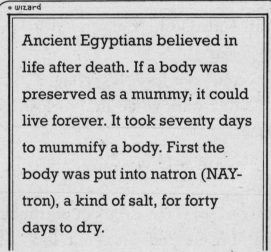

Ancient Egyptians believed in life after death. If a body was preserved as a mummy, it could live forever. It took seventy days to mummify a body. First the body was put into natron (NAY-tron), a kind of salt, for forty days to dry.

"Gross!" said Jess, making a face.

"No, it's not," said Josh. "It's cool."

Jess clicked to the next screen.

"Is there more?" asked Josh. Maybe there was a picture of a real mummy.

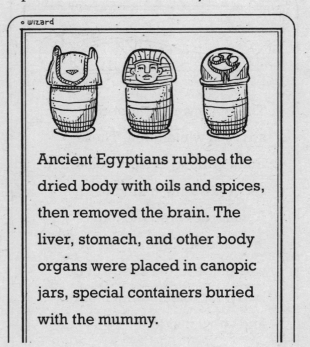

○ Wizard

Ancient Egyptians rubbed the dried body with oils and spices, then removed the brain. The liver, stomach, and other body organs were placed in canopic jars, special containers buried with the mummy.

"Are you kidding?" said Jess. It was really getting gross. She started to turn off the Wizard.

"Wait," said Josh. "We haven't gotten to the good part."

Jess clicked. There was a mummy on the next screen.

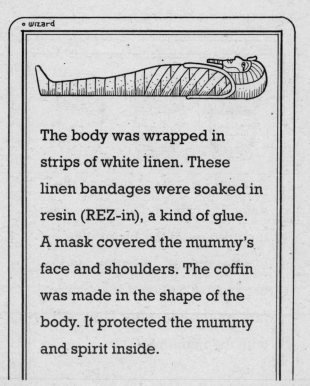

wizard

The body was wrapped in strips of white linen. These linen bandages were soaked in resin (REZ-in), a kind of glue. A mask covered the mummy's face and shoulders. The coffin was made in the shape of the body. It protected the mummy and spirit inside.

"Wow," said Josh. "The mask *is* important."

"Yeah," Jess agreed. She reached into Uncle

Harry's leather bag. Inside she felt the small golden statues. They were safe.

Suddenly, footsteps echoed from the dark hallway. Someone was coming.

Jess and Josh looked up.

"What's happening?" whispered Jess. She shoved the Wizard into the leather bag.

Her heart was racing. She moved closer to Josh.

"I'll check," said Josh. He peeked around the large clay jar.

A long dark shadow crossed the room. Josh made out the shape of a head. With a hat and ponytail.

Josh stood up.

"Over here!" he called out in a soft voice.

Uncle Harry crept over to the twins.

"No luck," he said. "The mask isn't here."

"Did you see a mummy?" asked Josh. He was excited.

Uncle Harry nodded. "Tutankhamun's

funeral begins at sunset. The workers are building three coffins. One coffin is put inside the next one. Tut's mummy is in a gold coffin. The one that goes inside the others."

Jess let out a long breath. "But where's the gold mask? The one with the missing statues?"

"The tomb," said Uncle Harry. "The mask must be there."

"Yeah," said Josh. "With all the other stuff he needs for the afterlife."

"How will we ever find the tomb?" Jess asked. There were lots of tombs dug into the cliff walls. Which one was Tut's?

Uncle Harry helped Jess up. "Don't worry," he said. "We'll figure out a way."

Slowly, they pushed open the heavy door of the funeral temple.

Standing outside was a big black dog with a jeweled collar.

"Nubis!" cried Jess. She rushed over and hugged her old friend.

"Awesome," said Uncle Harry.

Josh gave the dog a scratch behind the ears.

"His real name is *Anubis*," said their uncle. "Some say he is a god. A protector of the mummy. Anubis guides the spirit of the dead pharaoh to the next world."

Jess knelt down. She whispered into the dog's ear.

"Guide us," she said. "Show us Amun's tomb."

Nubis looked up and turned. He headed into the crowded road.

"Follow him!" said Uncle Harry.

Chapter 10

The Royal Tomb

"That way!" said Josh. There was a path just ahead.

Jess and Uncle Harry hurried to Josh's side.

They traveled west. Nubis led the way, toward the cliffs of the Valley of the Kings.

It was almost sunset. The tomb workers were returning to their homes. Some men carried picks and shovels on their shoulders. Other men led empty wagons. Work was done for the day.

The air over the desert was cool. Soon it would be dark. Stars would fill the sky.

"It's cold," said Jess. She wrapped her arms

around her body. Her feet were tired, too.

"We're almost there," said Uncle Harry. They were at the bottom of the highest cliff.

Nubis turned to the left and started to climb.

"He wants us to go that way," said Uncle Harry. He pointed to a narrow path cut into the face of the cliff. Jess and Josh gazed upward. The path went round and round, up the steep hill, to the top row of tombs.

"Wow!" said Josh, grabbing Jess's hand. They climbed slowly along the ledge of the cliff. They passed door after door of sealed tombs.

On the highest level, they stopped. Two soldiers guarded an open tomb.

"Shhh," whispered Uncle Harry. They hid behind a large stone column cut into the rock.

Nubis slipped past them along the cliff ledge. He sat at the soldiers' feet. Nubis looked up and stared into their eyes.

Jess held her breath.

"This is spooky," she whispered. The guards lowered their spears. They seemed to be in a trance.

Silently, Nubis stood up and walked in the opposite direction. As if they were dreaming, the guards left their post and followed the dog.

The twins watched from their hiding place. Nubis turned the corner. So did the guards. The dog disappeared just as mysteriously as he had appeared at the funeral temple.

The guards were gone.

"All clear!" cried Uncle Harry.

The twins rushed to the entrance of the tomb. Their uncle reached up and grabbed a wooden torch. The flame burned brightly.

"This is Tut's tomb," said Jess. She held up the blue stone necklace in the light. The cartouche matched the hieroglyphs carved above the door. *Tutankhamun.*

Uncle Harry nodded, leading the way.

They were in a large hall with a high ceiling.

A stone column was in each corner of the room. Another door was across from the tomb entrance.

"Wait," said Jess. "Let's check the Wizard." She searched for "the tomb of Tutankhamun" and read aloud.

○ Wizard

> The entrance to King Tut's tomb leads to a stairway; then there is a long passageway, slanting down. Another set of stairs and a second passageway lead to the antechamber. This room is filled with furniture, jewels, and gold treasures. The next room is the burial chamber. The king's mummy lies in the sarcophagus (sar-KAHF-a-gus), or stone coffin.

Uncle Harry was at the other door. He looked for a hidden lock.

"The passage to the burial chamber goes down, deep into the tomb," he said. "It's like the journey of the pharaoh through the underworld."

"Cool," said Josh. "What's there?"

"The pharaoh believes the underworld is filled with monsters," said Uncle Harry. "Lakes of fire, poisonous snakes, and other dangers."

Jess looked up. "Snakes?" She hated snakes!

"Oh, man," said Josh. "How did the ancient Egyptians ever get to the afterlife?"

Jess typed some keywords and clicked Search.

"Magic spells," said Jess. She read:

o wizard

Magic spells to protect the pharaohs were written on their coffins, on tomb walls, or on scrolls of papyrus. These spells were known as the *Book of the Dead.*

"Right," said Uncle Harry. "If you recited the correct spells, you could get past the bad stuff. That's what the ancient Egyptians believed."

"Cool!" said Josh. *More magic.*

Uncle Harry found the hidden lock. "Got it!"

The door swung open to reveal a stairway. Their uncle raised the torch. Slowly, they descended the stone steps.

Shadows from the torchlight bounced off the walls.

"This is creepy," said Josh. It was hard to see.

Jess kept her eyes at her feet — looking for snakes!

At the bottom of the steps, they came to a long hallway and then a second stairway. They walked down the steps, deeper into the tomb. The walls were covered with paintings of the pharaoh and his family.

"We must be close to the antechamber," said

Uncle Harry. "That room is filled with things that Tut needs in the afterlife."

Jess pointed to a painting on one wall. "Hey," she said. "There's a picture of Tut playing senet with his sister."

"And a hunting scene," said Josh, pointing to another painting. Tut was on his chariot with a spear in his hand.

"Let's see what's in the next room," said their uncle.

He pushed open the door to the ante-chamber.

Jess was the first to step in.

"Wow!" she said. The room was piled high with treasures. Furniture, clothes, jewelry, games, weapons, baskets of food . . .

Josh picked up a spear from the pile of weapons.

"Look at all this stuff," he said. He held the spear high above his shoulder. It was like the spear from the hippo hunt.

Jess reached down and grabbed a wooden figure. There were little carvings of people everywhere.

"Those are *shabtis*," said Uncle Harry. "Wooden models of servants."

"Why bury these with the pharaoh?" asked Jess. She held the figure in the light. It looked like a toy. There were hundreds. Some were servants. Others were farmers, soldiers, musicians, or carpenters.

"The ancient Egyptians had spells to bring the shabtis to life," explained their uncle. "They needed lots of servants to work the fields, cook the food, and do other jobs for the pharaoh in the next world."

"More magic spells," whispered Josh.

Uncle Harry pushed against the large door at the far end of the antechamber.

"This is it," he said. The twins followed him into the next room. It was the burial chamber.

"Awesome!" Uncle Harry raised the torch

higher. The walls were decorated with more beautiful paintings.

"Is that the sarcophagus?" asked Jess. She pointed to a large box in the center of the room. It was made of stone. Carvings covered the top and sides.

Their uncle nodded. "That's where Tut's mummy will be buried, in a gold coffin."

"I don't see the mask," said Josh. He looked around the chamber. The tomb was empty.

"Look behind the sarcophagus," said Uncle Harry. "It has to be here."

Jess heard a soft whimper. It came from a small room to the side of the burial chamber.

She walked over and peeked inside the room. A bright light was shining on a large black dog.

"Nubis," Jess gasped. He was resting on top of a golden chest.

The black dog leaped down. At his feet was Tut's golden mask.

"It's here!" Jess called over her shoulder.

Josh rushed over to the small room. Jess was trying to lift the golden mask. The dog was beside her.

"Uncle Harry," Josh cried. "We found the mask!"

Their uncle looked up from behind the sarcophagus. He heard noises. There were footsteps on the stairway. The sweet smell of incense drifted into the burial chamber.

It was Tut's funeral procession.

Uncle Harry raced to the small room to get Jess and Josh. He stopped. A smile spread across his face.

"Nubis!" their uncle said softly. Or was it Anubis, the jackal god? Had Tut's protector led them to the mask?

Uncle Harry reached into his leather bag and handed the golden statues to Jess. Josh helped him hold the golden mask.

"Hurry," Uncle Harry said. They were running out of time.

Jess clipped the snake and vulture figures to the headband. A perfect fit.

The mask was complete.

Chapter 11

Escape

The footsteps were getting louder.

Josh leaned against the big chest.

"Oh, man," he said. They were trapped in the small room.

"Is there another way out?" asked Jess. She looked around. All the walls were made of stone bricks.

"Look for a loose stone," said Uncle Harry. "Sometimes hidden passageways are built to trick the tomb robbers."

They moved their hands along the stones in the walls row by row, searching for a secret door.

Nubis stood up. Jess watched the dog walk to the far corner. With his nose, he touched a brick.

Jess saw it—a loose stone. She pushed the brick. A door swung open.

"Look," said Jess. It was another way out of the tomb.

"Good work," said Uncle Harry. He raised the torch and headed into the dark tunnel after Nubis. Jess turned to follow.

Josh grabbed her arm.

"Wait," he said. "Let's see the mummy."

Jess took a deep breath.

"Okay," she said. "Just a quick look."

The twins crouched down. They peeked from behind the secret door.

Two guards with flaming torches stepped into the burial chamber. More guards carried a golden coffin. It was shaped like a body.

"I bet Tut's mummy is inside," Josh whispered. He pointed to the coffin.

Jess stared at one of the guards. He was older now, but his mean face was the same.

"He's here!" said Jess softly. *The captain of the guards*.

They watched as servants pushed sleds with the canopic jars and more coffins into the burial chamber.

Jess looked over her shoulder. Uncle Harry was there.

"Hurry," whispered their uncle. "Nubis found the way out."

Josh pointed to the sarcophagus.

"Tut's mummy?" he asked.

Uncle Harry nodded. "They'll put the golden coffin inside the other coffins. The mummy mask, too. Three coffins altogether."

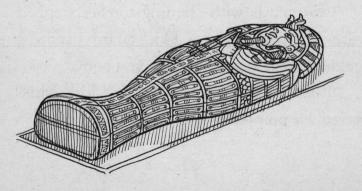

"Let's go," said their uncle, "while they put the lid on the sarcophagus." He stepped into the secret passageway.

Jess took one last look. Then her gaze met the eyes of the mean captain.

Jess froze. Did he see her, too?

A hand pulled her into the dark tunnel.

"Come on," whispered Josh.

"He saw me!" cried Jess. "I know it."

"Who?" Josh closed the door behind them.

"The captain." She was shaking.

Josh guided Jess away. They crept along the passageway.

Uncle Harry was ahead. "Be careful of the steps," he said, holding the torch high.

Jess kept looking at her feet—for snakes! She was falling behind.

"Come on, slowpoke," whispered Josh. He nudged his sister along the path.

Up and up they went on the narrow staircase. They felt along the walls as they climbed.

Jess looked back. No one was there.

Maybe the guard hadn't seen her after all.

Finally, they reached the entrance to the tomb.

People were waiting for the funeral procession to return. Uncle Harry took the lead. They walked through the crowd of mourners into the dark night.

Jess breathed in the fresh air. She looked around.

"Where's Nubis?"

"Gone," said their uncle.

Josh gazed above the cliffs. The sky was bright with stars.

"More magic," he said. Maybe the Egyptian god Anubis had saved them.

Uncle Harry led the twins behind a stone wall. He gathered them into his arms.

"Thank you," he said. "You were brave."

Jess looked up. "Can we go home now?"

Uncle Harry nodded. Then he handed his journal to Josh.

Jess and Josh watched as he set the hands of the time-compass.

"Wait," said Josh.

"We're done here," said their uncle. He was sending them home. Back to the attic in the big house in Boston.

"Are you coming with us, Uncle Harry?" asked Jess.

"No," he said. "I'll stay until the tomb is sealed. And I have to return the boat."

Josh wasn't ready to leave. "We can help."

"It's too dangerous," said their uncle. "Too many tomb robbers."

He looked at Jess. "And guards," he added.

"Please, Uncle Harry," said Josh.

Jess looked at her brother. Was he crazy? Hippo hunts. Mummies. Tomb robbers. It was time to go home.

Uncle Harry shook his head.

He turned the last hand of the time-compass into position.

"Ready?" asked their uncle.

Josh held the journal. Jess grabbed his other hand.

"Bye, Uncle Harry," the twins said together.

"Don't forget us," said Josh. "On your next adventure."

Uncle Harry smiled. The time-compass clicked louder and louder.

Jess and Josh closed their eyes.

A bright light cut across the dark sky.

In a sudden flash, they were back in the attic.

Chapter 12

Safe at Home

Heavy rain pounded against the attic windows. Josh and Jess stood next to the old trunk. Their Egyptian clothes were gone. Jess was wearing her shiny raincoat.

She opened her eyes slowly and dashed to a window.

Jess looked out. "We're home!" she said. It was about the same time as when they had left.

"Was it a dream?" asked Josh. "Or did we time travel with Uncle Harry to ancient Egypt?" The brown leather journal was in his hand.

"It was real," Jess said. She touched the blue stone on her neck.

"Poor Amun," Jess said sadly. She thought about the golden coffin. It was buried deep in the tomb in the Valley of the Kings. Tut's tomb.

Josh nodded. He remembered the mummy mask.

"He's on his way to the next life," said Josh. "And we helped."

"Do you think Uncle Harry is okay?" Jess asked in a soft voice.

"Remember the Wizard," said Josh. "What it said about Howard Carter? Everything was in the tomb when he opened it in 1922."

Jess pulled out the Wizard and searched for more information.

She stared at the screen. A frightened look came over her face.

"Well," said Josh, "what does it say about Tut's tomb?"

"Everything was there," Jess said. "The mask, too. But Carter was with another person. Lord Carnarvon."

Jess read:

Curse of the pharaoh: Some believe that whoever disturbs the mummy of an Egyptian pharaoh is placed under a curse and dies shortly afterward.

Josh looked puzzled. Was this a magic spell from ancient Egypt?

"There's more," said Jess.

Lord Carnarvon, who opened King Tut's tomb with Howard Carter, was bitten by a mosquito. He died later from an infection caused by the bite.

Jess was worried.

"Don't you see?" said Jess. "There's a curse on the tomb. Uncle Harry could be in trouble."

"Jess," Josh said. "The curse isn't real."

Josh looked at the journal in his hand.

"I bet Uncle Harry is off on another adventure right now."

Josh sat down next to the trunk. Jess moved beside him with the flashlight.

He found the map of Crete. Then he flipped through the pages about ancient Egypt.

There was a new map on the next page. Uncle Harry had left them a clue.

Jess leaned in closer. She pointed to a city on the map.

"Look," said Jess. "Ancient Rome."

Josh glanced at the city marked just below.

"Pompeii."

Jess looked up. "The ancient city buried by a volcano?"

Josh nodded. Was this their next time-travel adventure?

He closed the journal and put it into the trunk. Their uncle would return and leave the time-compass when he needed their help.

Jess took off the blue stone necklace. She laid it next to the journal. They had made a promise to Uncle Harry not to tell anyone about their time travels.

Slowly, Josh lowered the lid of the old trunk.

The rubber rain boots were standing next to the trunk. Jess handed a pair to Josh. Quickly, they pulled them on over their sneakers. It was time for school.

Josh was already at the attic door.

"Hurry, Jess," he shouted.

Jess took one last look at the old trunk.

"Coming."

She ran after Josh down the ladder.